Jerry Seinfeld's
HALLOWEEN

To my wonderful wife, Jessica, and our little Sascha, the sweetest candy of all.
—J.S.

To my favorite trick-or-treaters — Susan, Steven, and Brett.
—J.B.

This edition published by Little, Brown and Company exclusively for Hallmark Cards, Inc.
www.hallmark.com

This book has not been endorsed or sponsored by any of the candy companies whose
products are parodied and/or paid homage to in this book.

10 9 8 7 6 5 4 3

LEO-CHINA

Manufactured in China

BOK 6035

Jerry Seinfeld
Halloween

Illustrated by James Bennett

ISABELLA.

Timothy White

Jerry Seinfeld, the award-winning comedian, writer, and actor, starred for nine years in *Seinfeld*, one of the most acclaimed sitcoms of all time. The *New York Times* characterized his work as "keenly observed, carefully timed, contemplative humor about life's minutiae, people's foibles, and mankind's quotidian moments of angst." He is the author of a previous bestselling book for adults, *Seinlanguage*, and is the subject of a new documentary about comedy. He resides in New York with his wife, Jessica, and their young daughter, Sascha.

James Bennett has illustrated for many major publications, including *Time, Sports Illustrated, BusinessWeek*, and *Mad* magazine. Last year he received the Hamilton King Award from the Society of Illustrators for Best Illustration of the Year. He lives and works in Bucks County, Pennsylvania, with his wife, Susan, and their two young sons, Steven and Brett. James's most lasting memory of Halloween was when he went trick-or-treating as Shirley Temple.

A Byron Preiss Book

Jerry Seinfeld
Halloween
Illustrated by James Bennett

A Byron Preiss Book

Little, Brown and Company

Boston   New York   London

When you're a kid you can eat amazing amounts of food.
All I ate when I was a kid was candy. Just candy, candy, candy.
And the only really clear thought I had as a kid was *get candy.*

GET CANDY,

GET CANDY,

GET CANDY,

GET CANDY.

Family, friends, school—
they were just obstacles in the way
of getting more candy.

So the first time you hear the concept of Halloween when you're a kid, your brain can't even process the idea.

You're like, "What is this? What did you say? Someone's giving out candy? Who's giving out candy?

EVERYONE WE KNOW

is just *giving out* candy?

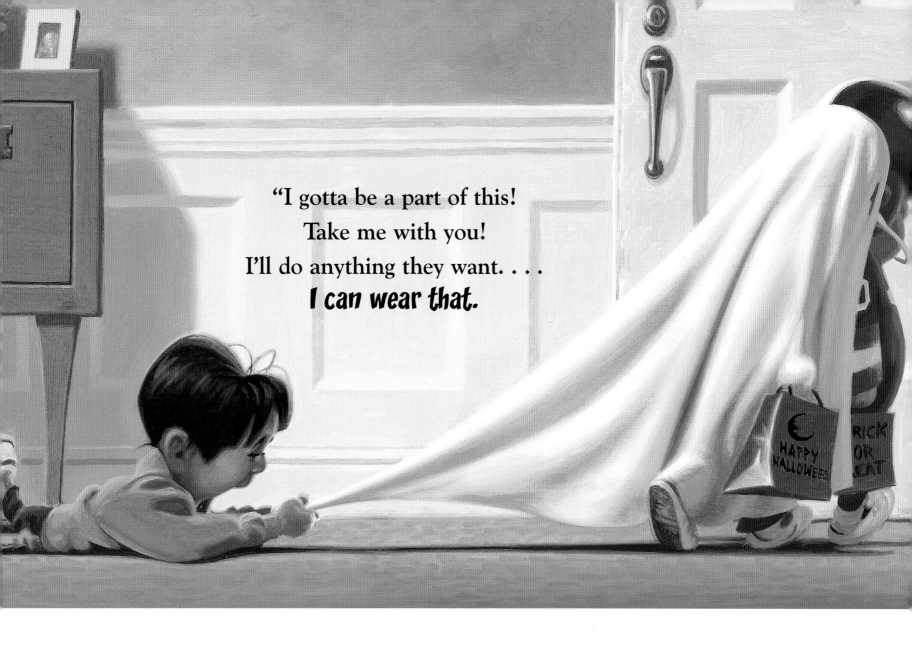

"I gotta be a part of this!
Take me with you!
I'll do anything they want. . . .
I can wear that.

I'll wear anything I have to wear.
I'll do anything I have to do
to get the candy from those
fools who are so stupidly **giving it away.**"

The first couple of years I made my own costumes.
Ghost, hobo . . . the worst.

I knew my destiny was to one day get a real Superman Halloween costume from the store. You know the one. . . . The cardboard box . . . the cellophane top . . . mask included in the set . . .

Oh, BABY!

Remember the rubber band on the back of those masks?

That was a quality item. Thinnest gray rubber in the world. It was good for about ten seconds before it snapped out of that cheap little staple they put it in there with. You go to the first house, "Trick or . . . SNAP! It broke, I don't believe it!

"Wait up! I got to fix it. You guys, wait up!"
Kids don't want other kids to wait, they want them to wait *up*.
"Would you *wait up?*"

Because when you're little, your whole life is up.
You want to grow up. Everything is up!

"Wait UP!"

"Hold UP!"

"Shut UP!"

"Mom, I'll clean UP. . . .

Just let me stay UP!"

When you're a parent it's just the opposite:
Everything is down.
"Just calm down!"

"Slow **DOWN!**"

"Sit **DOWN!**"

"Come **DOWN** here!"

"Put that **DOWN!**"

"And keep it **DOWN** in there!"

"You're **GROUNDED!**"

So the day finally came. I finally convinced my parents to buy me an official **Superman** Halloween-store costume.

I was physically ready. I was mentally prepared. And I absolutely believed when I put this costume on that I would look *exactly* like the **Superman** I had come to know on television and in the movies.

Unfortunately, these costumes are not exactly the **super fit** that you are hoping for.

You look more like you're wearing Superman's pajamas.

It's all loose and flowy, the **neckline** comes down to about your stomach.

You got that **flimsy** little ribbon string in the back holding it all together.

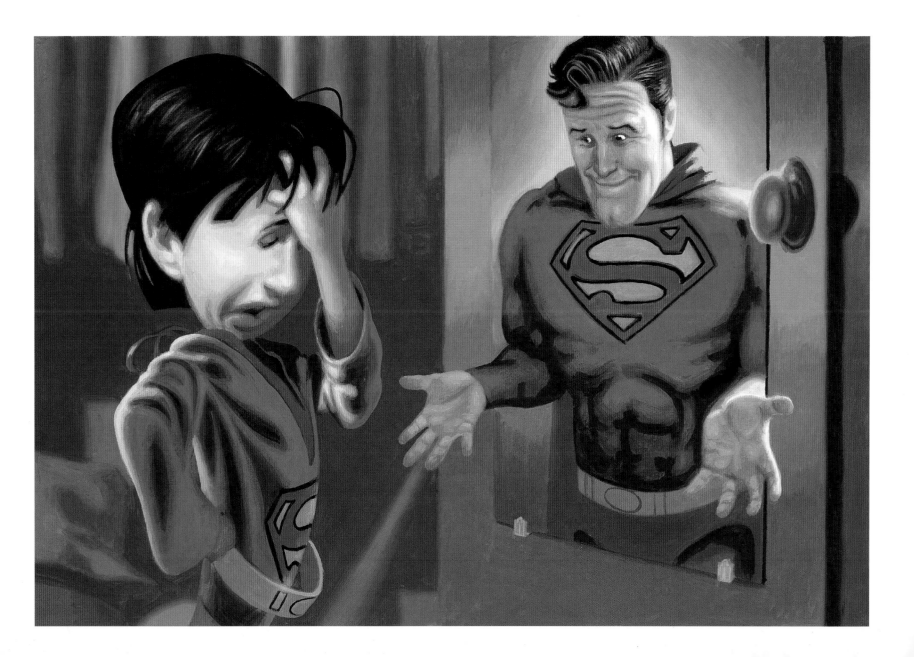

Plus my mother makes me wear my **winter coat** over the costume anyway.

I don't recall Superman
wearing a JACKET.
I read every comic book.
I do not remember him ever once
flying with a coat on.
Not like the one I had—
cheap corduroy, phony fur.

So you go out anyway and the mask keeps breaking,
the rubber band keeps getting shorter
because you need to keep **retying it.**

It's getting tighter and tighter on your face.
Now you can't even **see!**

You're trying to breathe through that little hole that gets all sweaty.

Whoosh, whoosh.

The mask starts slicing into your eyeballs.

"I can't see, I can't breathe.
But let's keep going.
We gotta get the candy!"

About half an hour into trick-or-treating you take that mask off.

"Oh, the heck with it!"

Year after year, I never gave
up on trick-or-treating.
But I remember those
last few Halloweens.

I was getting a little
too old for it. . . .
I was just kinda going through
the motions.
Bing-BONG
"Come on lady, let's go!
Halloween, doorbells, candy,
let's pick it up in there."

They come to the door; they always ask
you the same stupid question.
"What are *you* supposed to be?"

"I'm supposed to be *done* by now.
You want to move it along with the 3Musketeers®?

Sometimes people give you the little white bag, twisted on the top.
You know that's gonna be some CRUMMY candy.
"No **official Halloween** markings on it?
I don't think so."

"Wait a second, what is this? The orange marshmallow shaped like a big peanut?

"Do me a favor,
you keep that one.
We've got all the
doorstops we need already,
thank you very much.
We're going for
name candy only
this year."

At the end of Halloween
I was able to fill a punch bowl
so full of candy that the top
of it would be curved.
It was like a planet.